Richard Scarry's
Busy Day Storybooks

The Firefighters' Busy Day

J.B. COMMUNICAT

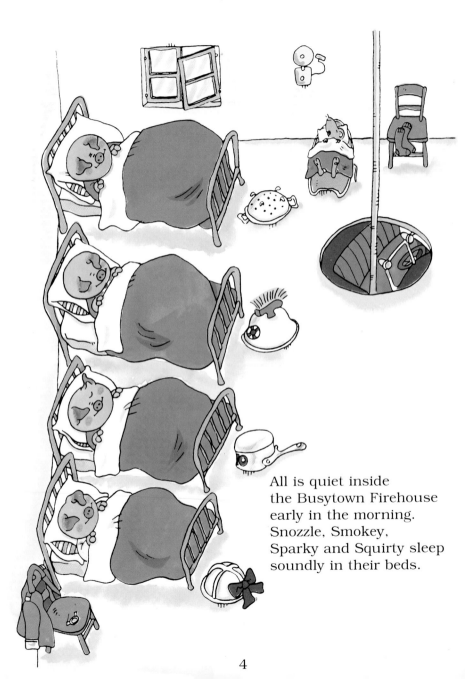

All is quiet inside
the Busytown Firehouse
early in the morning.
Snozzle, Smokey,
Sparky and Squirty sleep
soundly in their beds.

4

"Drrinnng!!!"
sounds the fire alarm.

The four firefighters jump from
their beds, put on their helmets,
and slide down the pole.
The fire engine waits downstairs.

Hurry,
firefighters!

5

The fire engine races through the streets.
"Clang! Clang!" goes the bell.
"Toot! Toot!" sounds Sparky's horn.

Make way, everybody!

6

They arrive at
Mr. Frumble's
house.
My! Look at all
that smoke!

7

Smokey, Sparky, Squirty and Snozzle burst through the door, fire hose in hand.

Mr. Frumble is preparing burnt toast for breakfast. Yum. Yum.

The firefighters drive back to the firehouse and sit down for breakfast.

Smokey prepares pancakes.

"Drrinnng!!!" sounds the alarm again.

Sorry, firefighters! Breakfast will have to wait!

Off drive
the firefighters
to the rescue.

It's Mr. Frumble again.
His pickle car key
has fallen into
the gutter.
Smokey pulls it out
with a magnet.

The firefighters return
to the firehouse
to eat cold pancakes.

"Drrinnng!!!" sounds the alarm
once again.

The firetruck speeds once again
to the rescue.

Guess who
needs help?
Mr. Frumble
should learn
to drive more
carefully, don't
you think?

Smokey turns off the fire hydrant, and Mr. Frumble and his pickle car land softly on the street.

The firefighters return to the firehouse.

They decide to grill hot dogs.

"Drrinnng!!!" goes the alarm.

12

The firefighters race
to the rescue again.

Uh-oh. Now
Mr. Frumble
has lost his
hat in a tree.

Using a ladder, the firefighters fetch Mr. Frumble's hat and give it back to him.

"Drrinnng! Drrinnng!" goes the telephone on the firetruck. Smokey answers the phone. It's another alarm.

It's a FIRE!

14

The firefighters
hurry through the streets.

"Clang! Clang!"
"Toot! Toot!"
Watch out,
everybody!

15

Smoke billows out of a garage door. Squirty shoots
the water cannon. Sparky runs forward with the hose.
Hurry, firefighters!

"Whooosh!!!" With a spray of water,
the fire is out in an instant.

Good work, firefighters! Uh-oh. It was the firefighters' hot dogs.

I think you will have to find something else to eat.

"Drrinnng!" sounds the alarm.

Without wasting a minute,
the firefighters are off
to the next emergency.
Poor, hungry firefighters!

They arrive at Mr. Frumble's house again.
Mr. Frumble is having a bath.

I think your bathtub is full now, Mr. Frumble.

So that they can finally have a quiet moment
to eat, the firefighters invite Mr. Frumble to
have dinner with them at the firehouse.

Squirty stirs a big pot of firefighter stew.

Sparky brings out the bowls.

Everyone sits down at the table. Doesn't the stew smell good!

"Drrinnng!!!" goes the alarm.

The firefighters are off to the next rescue.
My, don't firefighters have a busy day!

Oh, bon appétit, Mr. Frumble!

FINES
5¢ PER DAY
FOR
OVERDUE BOOKS